C000060692

WHEN MOM TRAVELS
FOR WORK

KRISTOPHER JAMES GOEDEN

Illustrated by CSILLA SZEGEDI

For Krew and Slater: There's nowhere else in the world I'd rather be than with you boys. Love, Dad

To request permissions, contact the publisher at Unlessventuresllc@gmail.com

Publisher's Cataloguing-in-Publication Data
Names: Goeden, Kristopher, author. | Szegedi, Csilla, illustrator.
Title: When mom travels for work / by Kristopher James Goeden ; illustrated by Csilla Szegedi
Description: First edition. | Urbandale, IA ; Unless Ventures [2023] | Summary: This story told in rhyming text explains to children why a mom may need to leave home for work and what they can do to help the family while that parent is away.
Identifiers: LCCN 2023902925 | ISBN 979-8-9869406-8-7 (hardcover) | ISBN 979-8-9869406-9-4 (paperback) | ISBN 979-8-9869406-7-0 (ebook)
Subjects: | CYAC: Stories in rhyme - Fiction | Family life - Fiction | Travel - Fiction | Schools - Fiction | Work and family - Fiction.
Classification: LCC PZ8.3.G64346 Whe 2023 | DDC [E] - dc23

Book design and Illustrations by Csilla Szegedi

Printed in the United States

First Edition

Published by Unless Ventures
Urbandale, IA
www.UnlessVenturesLLC.com

WHEN MOM TRAVELS
FOR WORK

KRISTOPHER JAMES GOEDEN
Illustrated by CSILLA SZEGEDI

Before you woke up,
Mom had to be gone.

She whispered goodbye as she left
BEFORE DAWN.

Mom needs to travel and work
FAR AWAY,

while you stay at home and begin your
NEW DAY.

When you were at school, she soared up above.

No matter the distance, she sends you her **LOVE**.

While Mommy's away, she'll be sure to **WORK HARD**.

MOM DESIGN

She hopes you'll have fun
PLAYING GAMES
in the yard.

Mom goes to work to make money, you see,

to buy things we need —
SINCE FOOD ISN'T FREE.

While Mom's off at work, we all must pitch in.
Completing your chores would be
A BIG WIN!

When Mom's not at home,
please keep in mind

to be helpful, supportive,

AND MOST OF ALL, KIND.

Each night in your dreams,
Mom hopes that you'll roam,

then share your adventures

WHEN SHE RETURNS HOME.

Mom may have to travel and work quite a lot,

but smile and know
FAMILY'S HER ONE FAVORITE THOUGHT.

And once she comes back,
she wants, far and above,

to care for her family with
ALL OF HER LOVE.

So please don't be sad when Mommy leaves home.

She's with you in spirit.

YOU'RE NEVER ALONE.

MOMMY
LOVES YOU.

Printed in Great Britain
by Amazon

23856838R00021